Hugger, _n._, one who hugs —Ant., huggee [Obs.] a person or thing that receives a hug

Huggable, _adj._, possessing an affectionate nature or qualities desirable to hug —Ant., unhuggable

A Book of Hugs

by Dave Ross
illustrated by Laura Rader

HARPERCOLLINSPUBLISHERS

For Mom & Dad
(who taught me how to hug) —D.R.

For my "sister" Lyn, expert at the
single-arm hug, with love —L.R.

A Book of Hugs
Text copyright © 1980, 1999 by Dave Ross
Illustrations copyright © 1999 by Laura Rader
Printed in the U.S.A. All rights reserved.
http://www.harperchildrens.com

Library of Congress Cataloging-in-Publication Data
Ross, Dave, 1949–
    A book of hugs / by Dave Ross ; illustrated by Laura Rader.
        p.   cm.
    Summary: Describes a variety of hugs, including people hugs, blanket hugs,
and birthday hugs, and presents facts and hints about hugs.
    ISBN 0-06-028147-2
    [1. Hugging—Fiction.]   I. Rader, Laura, ill.   II. Title.
PZ7.R71964Bo   1999   98-18659
[E]—dc21   CIP
                                                                        AC

Typography by Al Cetta
3 4 5 6 7 8 9 10
❖
Newly Illustrated Edition

There are all kinds of hugs in the world. . . .

PUPPY HUGS

Puppy hugs are very soft and wet.

BEAR HUGS

Bear hugs are very strong. Be careful not to hurt.

OCTOPUS HUGS

An octopus hugs with its whole body.

FISH HUGS

Fish hugs are very cold and seldom returned.

P.S. Never hug a shark.

PORCUPINE HUGS

Porcupine hugs are done very carefully.

FRAIDYCAT HUGS

Fraidycat hugs make you feel safe.

PIGGYBACK HUGS

Sometimes called riding piggyback.

A good way to travel or see a parade.

MOMMY HUGS

You can never hug a Mommy too much.

DADDY HUGS

Daddy hugs are best when he first walks in the door.

BROTHER HUGS

Usually called a buddy hug.

Note: A circle of buddy huggers is called a huddle.

GRANDPA HUGS

Grandpa hugs are sometimes given while sitting.

GRANDMA HUGS

Grandma hugs can be found anywhere, but are especially nice in the kitchen.

SISTER HUGS

Also known as a single-arm hug.

Single-arm hugs are good for when you
walk together
(even if you aren't sisters).

BABY HUGS

Baby hugs are given with a little tickle.

GREAT-AUNT MARY HUGS

A Great-Aunt Mary hug can be given
only once a year.

(You will usually end up with lipstick on your cheek.)

ARM HUGS

Arm hugs are good if you are too little to get
your arms around someone.

HAND HUGS
Usually called shaking hands.

Never hand-hug with dirty hands
unless you both have dirty hands.

KNEE HUGS

Knee hugs are good if you are tall.

Warning:
Never try
to knee-hug
someone who
is moving.

BLANKET HUGS

Everyone needs some kind of blanket.

ROCK HUGS

Rock hugs are very hard on your face.

ICE-CUBE HUGS

Ice-cube hugs are quite common in February.

LAMPPOST HUGS

A lamppost hug can save you from
a painful experience.

SANDWICH HUGS

The whole family can get into a sandwich hug.

BIRTHDAY HUGS

A birthday hug is a present anyone can afford.

REPORT CARD HUGS

A Hug

Bee Hug

Sea Hug

HURT HUGS

Hurt hugs make the pain go away.

GOOD-NIGHT HUGS

Also sleep-tight and don't-let-the-bedbugs-bite hugs.

All hugs are wonderful, but
the best hugs of all are . . . .

I-love-you hugs.

FACTS & HINTS ABOUT HUGGING

There is no such thing as a bad hug: there are only good hugs and great hugs.

Hug someone at least once a day and twice on a rainy day.

Hug with a smile; closed eyes are optional.